To Ethan, for all his adventures in the woods.

First published in Great Britain in 2019 by Andersen Press Ltd.,
20 Vauxhall Bridge Road, London SW1V 2SA.
Copyright © Robert Starling 2019.
The right of Robert Starling to be identified as the author
and illustrator of this work has been asserted by him in
accordance with the Copyright, Designs and Patents Act, 1988.
All rights reserved.
Printed and bound in China.
1 3 5 7 9 10 8 6 4 2
British Library Cataloguing in Publication Data available.
ISBN 978 1 78344 848 7

ROBERT STARLING

FERGAL IN A FIX!

ANDERSEN PRESS

Look, it's Fergal!

He's a happy
little fellow...

except today he's off
to Dragon Camp

and he's feeling
a bit worried.

"You'll meet lots of other dragons there," said Dad.

"You'll try things you've never done before," explained Mum.

Still, Fergal was fretting. "I hope everyone likes me at Dragon Camp," he thought. "Perhaps if I'm the best at everything..."

When they got to the camp, Fergal couldn't believe his eyes!

There were dragons everywhere! Tall ones, spiky ones, bright ones – even feathered ones.

"Come and meet the others," said the jolly camp leader,
"and then we'll get started."

The first activity was
fire breathing.

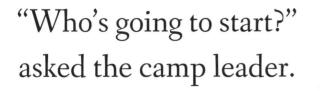

"Who's going to start?"
asked the camp leader.

Fergal rushed to be first in line.

"Watch this!" said Fergal. "I'm great at flaming."

Fergal tried really hard...

But he wasn't the best.

So when they started lair-building,
Fergal was anxious to do better.

He looked for all the best sticks.

FLOMP!

OI!

WHAT A CHEEK.

He didn't get his lair finished... but everyone else seemed to be having trouble, too.

Then there was a treasure hunt!

Fergal was determined to be the best treasure hunter.

He was the first to find the treasure. Although the others didn't seem very happy about it.

HOW DID HE GET THERE?

The last activity of the morning was camp cooking.

Fergal felt confident; he'd
baked bread at home.

In fact, he showed the
others how it was done.

But when the bread was ready, nobody seemed that keen to eat it.

Then it was lunchtime and Fergal found himself all alone.

He felt there must be something wrong...

Why weren't the others being friendly?

The leader spotted Fergal looking glum.
"What's the matter, Fergal?" he asked.

"Everything's gone wrong," snuffled Fergal, "I wanted
to make friends and be good at everything.

I'm not the best at flaming. I couldn't
get my lair right. I found the treasure,
but everyone glared at me,
nobody ate my bread
and now they
won't sit with
me."

"There's an easy way to get out of this fix, Fergal,"
suggested the leader. "Maybe you're trying too hard.
You don't have to be the best at the activities.
You just need to be the best **you**."

Fergal thought
about this.

And that's what he did: he stopped trying to beat everyone and he fixed it.

He made friends.

He shared his snacks.

He didn't lead, but he pulled
his weight in the team.

GREAT ROWING, FERGAL.

Fergal's worries seemed far away
by the end of Camp. He wasn't
the best at anything...

... except being Fergal.

And that's the best anyone can be.